Happy Birthday, DANNY and the DINOSAUR!

Story and Pictures by
SYD HOFF

HarperCollins*Publishers*

Happy Birthday, Danny and the Dinosaur!
Copyright © 1995 by Syd Hoff
Printed in the U.S.A. All rights reserved.

Library of Congress Cataloging-in-Publication Data
Hoff, Syd, date
  Happy birthday, Danny and the dinosaur! / story and pictures by
Syd Hoff.
      p.   cm. — (An I can read book)
  Summary: Six-year-old Danny invites his dinosaur friend to come to
his birthday party.
  ISBN 0-06-026437-3. — ISBN 0-06-026438-1 (lib. bdg.)
  [1. Dinosaurs—Fiction. 2. Birthdays—Fiction.] I. Title. II. Series.
PZ7.H672Had   1995   95-2710
[E]—dc20   CIP
                                                                  AC

1 2 3 4 5 6 7 8 9 10
❖
First Edition

For Bonnie

Danny was in a hurry.

He had to see his friend

the dinosaur.

5

"I'm six years old today,"

said Danny.

"Will you come

to my birthday party?"

"I would be delighted,"

said the dinosaur.

Danny rode the dinosaur

out of the museum.

On the way

they picked up Danny's friends.

"Today I'm a hundred million years

and one day old," said the dinosaur.

10

"Then it can be your party too!"

said Danny.

11

The children helped Danny's father

hang up balloons.

"See, I can help too,"

said the dinosaur.

Danny's mother gave out party hats.

"How do I look?"

asked the dinosaur.

15

"We would like to sing a song,"

said a girl and a boy.

16

They sang,

and everybody clapped their hands.

"I can sing too," said the dinosaur.

He sang,

and everybody covered their ears.

19

"Let's play pin the tail

on the donkey," said Danny.

The dinosaur pinned the tail

on himself!

The children sat down to rest.

"Please don't put your feet

on the furniture," said Danny.

The dinosaur put his feet

out the window.

Danny's mother and father

gave each child

a dish of ice cream.

They had to give the dinosaur
more!

"Here comes the birthday cake!"

said the children.

They counted the candles.

"One, two, three, four, five, six."

The dinosaur started to eat

the cake.

"Wait!" said Danny.

"First we have to make a wish!"

"I wish we can all be together again
next year," said Danny.
"I wish the same thing,"
said the dinosaur.

They blew out the candles.

"Happy birthday to you!"

everybody sang.

31

"This is the best birthday party
I have ever had," said Danny.
"Me too," said the dinosaur.

ML